U.S. NATIONAL PARKS

YELLOWSTONE NATIONAL PARK

by Penelope S. Nelson

pogo

Ideas for Parents and Teachers

Pogo Books let children practice reading informational text while introducing them to nonfiction features such as headings, labels, sidebars, maps, and diagrams, as well as a table of contents, glossary, and index.

Carefully leveled text with a strong photo match offers early fluent readers the support they need to succeed.

Before Reading

- "Walk" through the book and point out the various nonfiction features. Ask the student what purpose each feature serves.
- Look at the glossary together. Read and discuss the words.

Read the Book

- Have the child read the book independently.
- Invite him or her to list questions that arise from reading.

After Reading

- Discuss the child's questions. Talk about how he or she might find answers to those questions.
- Prompt the child to think more. Ask: What did you know about Yellowstone National Park before reading this book? What more would you like to learn about it?

Pogo Books are published by Jump!
5357 Penn Avenue South
Minneapolis, MN 55419
www.jumplibrary.com

Library of Congress Cataloging-in-Publication Data

Names: Nelson, Penelope, 1994- author.
Title: Yellowstone National Park / by Penelope S. Nelson.
Description: Minneapolis, MN: Jump!, Inc., [2020]
Series: U.S. national parks
Includes index.
Audience: Ages 7-10.
Identifiers: LCCN 2018055798 (print)
LCCN 2018056957 (ebook)
ISBN 9781641288163 (ebook)
ISBN 9781641288156 (hardcover : alk. paper)
Subjects: LCSH: Yellowstone National Park
Juvenile literature.
Classification: LCC F722 (ebook)
LCC F722.N45 2020 (print)
DDC 978.7/52–dc23
LC record available at https://lccn.loc.gov/2018055798

Editor: Jenna Trnka
Designer: Jenna Casura

Photo Credits: alptraum/iStock, cover; Kenneth Keifer/Shutterstock, 1; f11photo/Shutterstock, 3; Bertl123/Shutterstock, 4; cumulus_humilis/iStock, 5; Lorcel/Shutterstock, 6-7; JREden/iStock, 8-9; NicolasMcComber/iStock, 10; Varina C/Shutterstock, 11; Riishede/iStock, 12-13; ABC Collection/Alamy, 14-15; Jason Patrick Ross/Shutterstock, 16-17; Werner Forman/Getty, 18; Birdiegal/Shutterstock, 19; NPS Photo/Alamy, 20-21; Nagel Photography/Shutterstock, 23.

Printed in the United States of America at Corporate Graphics in North Mankato, Minnesota.

TABLE OF CONTENTS

CHAPTER 1

ATOP A VOLCANO

Would you like to see huge **geysers**? Or see waterfalls in a **canyon**?

Maybe you want to see mud pots. These are pools of hot, bubbling mud! Welcome to Yellowstone National Park!

The park is in three states. Most of it is in Wyoming. Parts are in Montana and Idaho. A volcano sits beneath it. This is what created the geysers. See **hot springs**. There are **steam vents**, too.

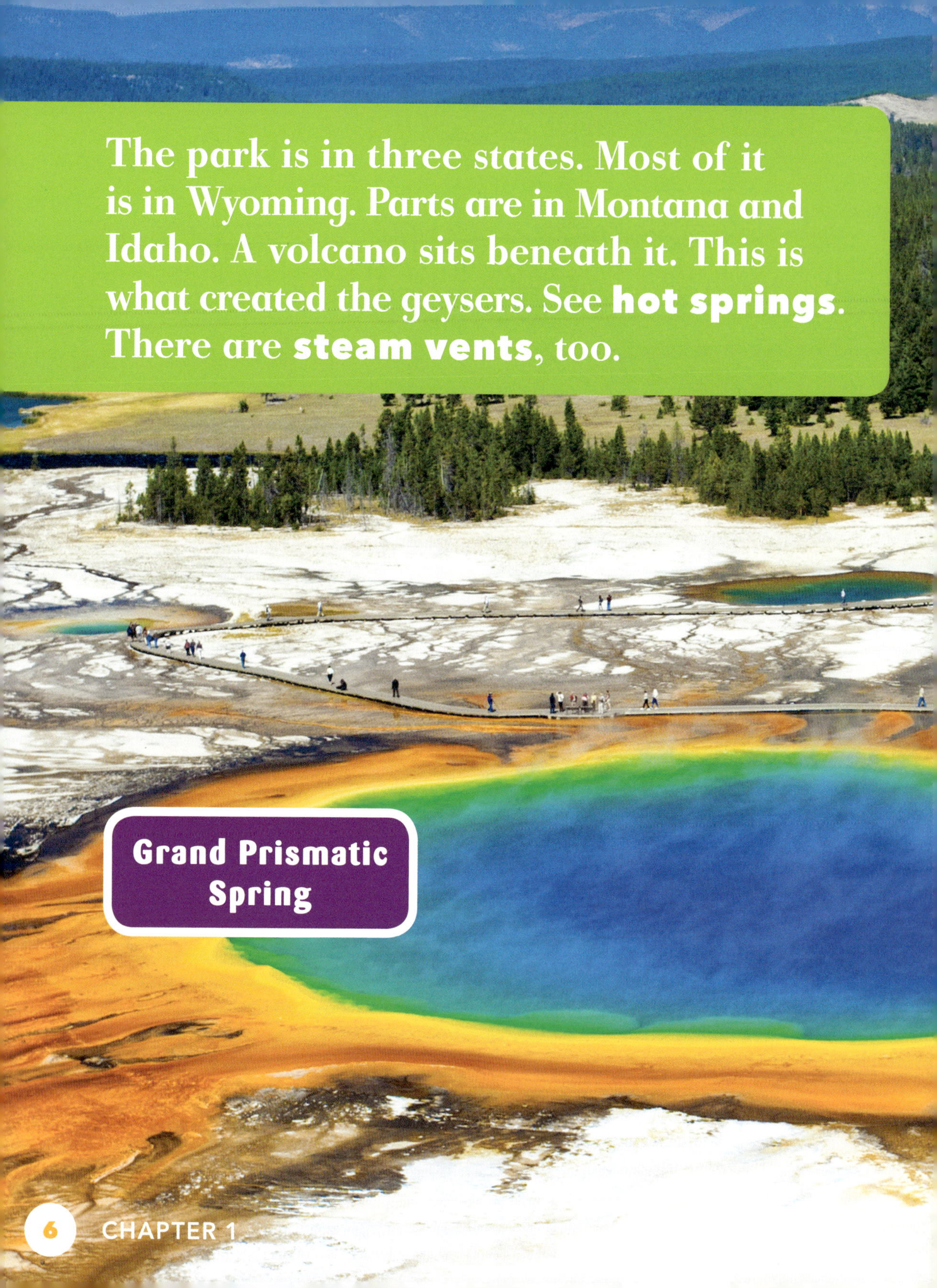

Grand Prismatic Spring

TAKE A LOOK!

The volcano erupted about 640,000 years ago. It made a **caldera**. **Magma** is close to Earth's surface.

■ = Earth's crust
■ = caldera
■ = geyser
■ = partially molten crust
■ = magma

This unique area is home to many animals. You could see grizzly and black bears. Elk and moose roam. Lakes and rivers are home to otters and beavers. Hayden Valley is a great place to spot bison.

WHAT DO YOU THINK?

The bison in the park almost went **extinct**. Why? People hunted too many. By the early 1900s, there were only about 25 left. The government made hunting them illegal. This helped save them. Do you think this was a good idea? Why or why not?

Hayden Valley

CHAPTER 2

WONDERS OF THE PARK

Hot springs created the **terraces** at Mammoth Hot Springs. Hot water flows over the terraces. **Minerals** build up. Special **bacteria** give areas color. Boardwalks allow people to explore!

Dip your toes in Yellowstone Lake. This lake is too cold for swimming. But it has 141 miles (227 kilometers) of shoreline to explore! The **climate** of this park changes with the seasons. The water is cold even in the summer because of the high **altitude**.

Watch Old Faithful erupt. This is the most famous geyser in the park. It goes off about every hour or hour and a half. Water shoots at least 100 feet (30 meters) into the air. Some blasts reach 180 feet (55 m)!

DID YOU KNOW?

Scientists study Old Faithful's eruptions. This helps them **predict** when it will erupt next. They can predict how high the water will shoot, too! They can't predict perfectly. But they get closer all the time!

Old Faithful

Steamboat
Geyser

Head to the Norris Geyser Basin. You can see Steamboat Geyser. It is the tallest geyser in the world! It blasts 300 to 400 feet (91 to 122 m) into the air!

Did you know Yellowstone has its own Grand Canyon? There are many hiking trails around the rim. Go to Artist Point. It is on the edge of a cliff. It offers the best view of the canyon!

Grand Canyon of the Yellowstone

CHAPTER 3

HUMAN IMPACT

People have lived in this area for more than 10,000 years! Native Americans made their own tools. Many were made from **obsidian** found in Obsidian Cliff.

obsidian knife

There are many buildings and monuments to see. Some are almost as old as the park itself! This is the arch at the North Entrance. President Theodore Roosevelt laid the first stone in 1903.

Many people work in the park. They protect it. They study its **geology**. Would you like to learn more about the park? You can! Talk to a park ranger. Rangers lead hikes, too.

Yellowstone is an amazing place! What do you want to see first?

WHAT DO YOU THINK?

Yellowstone was the first national park. It was founded in 1872. The government runs these parks. They protect the land, animals, and plants in them. Do you think this is important? Why or why not?

park ranger

QUICK FACTS & TOOLS

AT A GLANCE

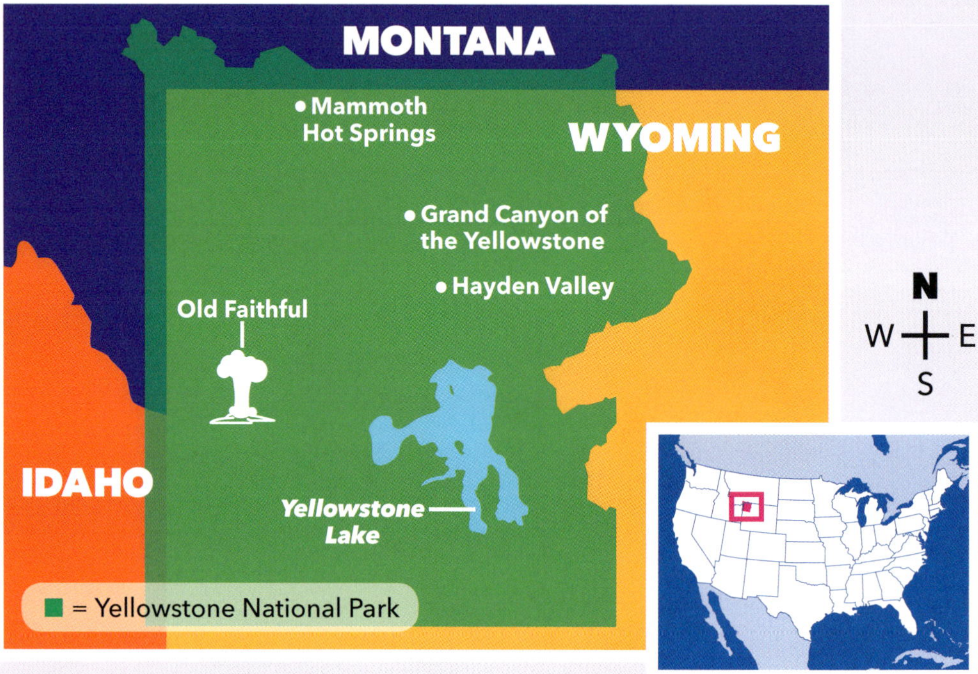

YELLOWSTONE NATIONAL PARK

Location: Wyoming, Montana, Idaho

Year Established: 1872

Area: 2,221,766 acres (899,117 hectares)

Approximate Yearly Visitors: 3.5 million

Top Attractions: Mammoth Hot Springs, Old Faithful, Yellowstone Lake

GLOSSARY

altitude: The height of something above sea level.

bacteria: Tiny, single-celled living things that exist everywhere.

caldera: A large crater formed after a major volcanic eruption.

canyon: A deep, narrow valley with steep sides and often a river running through it.

climate: The weather typical of a place over a long period of time.

extinct: No longer found alive.

geology: The study of Earth's physical structure, especially its layers of soil and rock.

geysers: Underground hot springs that shoot boiling water and steam into the air.

hot springs: Natural sources of hot water that flow from the ground.

magma: Melted rock found beneath Earth's surface that becomes lava when it flows out of volcanoes.

minerals: Solid substances found in Earth that don't come from animals or plants.

obsidian: A dark, natural glass formed by the cooling of molten lava.

predict: To say what will happen in the future.

steam vents: Holes in a volcanic region from which hot gases and vapors rise.

terraces: Raised, flat platforms with sloping sides.

INDEX

TO LEARN MORE

Finding more information is as easy as 1, 2, 3.

1. Go to www.factsurfer.com
2. Enter "YellowstoneNationalPark" into the search box.
3. Choose your book to see a list of websites.

FACT SURFER